Dear Parent;

As parents we may find ourselves trying to explain to our children what we do during the day. My own daughter told her teacher she wasn't sure what I did, but it had something to do with books!

I Can Read books are designed for beginning readers to take their first independent steps. This delightful book is one that will hold their interest, as well as provide a text that will ensure success for the fledgling reader. *Frida's Office Day* shows young Frida Cat spending a day at work with her father. With boundless energy and resourcefulness, young Frida gets first hand knowledge of what her own father does for a job.

We recommend reading the book all the way through with your child, so that he or she gets a sense of the story. Then, let your child try to read.

Be patient. Try to remember what learning to read was like. Give positive reinforcement. Even reading just a word or two is great progress for a beginning reader.

Be a good listener. As you know, you need your audience to listen carefully when you are reading a story. Offer the same undivided attention.

Show your appreciation. Reading is more fun when it is truly enjoyed. Laugh at all the right places. When you say "thank you" to your reader, your child will feel important.

We hope this (and other) I Can Read books have a valued place in your home.

Sincerely,

Stephen Fraser

Stephen Fraser
Senior Editor
Weekly Reader Book Club

An I Can Read Book®

FRIDA'S
OFFICE DAY

by Thomas P. Lewis
pictures by Doug Cushman

HarperCollins Publishers

This book is a presentation of Newfield Publications, Inc.
Newfield Publications offers book clubs for children
from preschool through high school. For further
information write to: **Newfield Publications, Inc.,**
4343 Equity Drive, Columbus, Ohio 43228.

Published by arrangement with HarperCollins Publishers.
Newfield Publications is a trademark of Newfield
Publications, Inc. I Can Read Book is a
registered trademark of HarperCollins Publishers.

Library of Congress Cataloging-in-Publication Data
Lewis, Thomas P.
    Frida's office day / by Thomas P. Lewis; pictures by Doug
Cushman. — 1st ed.
        p.   cm. — (An I can read book)
    Summary: Frida Cat goes in to work with her father,
spends the morning helping him in his office,
and has a fun afternoon with him enjoying the big city.
    ISBN 0-06-023843-7:$ ISBN 0-06-023844-5 (lib. bdg.):
$
    [1. Cats — Fiction 2. Work — Fiction. 3. City and town life —
Fiction. 4. Father and daughters — Fiction.] I. Cushman, Doug,
ill. II. Title. III. Series.

PZ7.L5882Fr 1989   87-33488
[E]—dc19   CIP
                                                  AC

"Rise and shine, Frida mine,"

called Mr. Cat.

"Get ready to work, work, work!"

Frida jumped out of bed.

"Okay, Boss," she said.

It was school vacation.

Frida was going to help her father

at his office in the city.

"I just have to put on

my work clothes," said Frida.

Frida dressed up in a blue blouse,

a skirt with big pockets,

a necklace

and three bracelets.

"Hurry up, Frida," called Mrs. Cat.

"You don't want to miss your train."

Frida ate breakfast standing up,

just like her mother and father.

"Time to go," said Mr. Cat.

"Good-bye, Mommy," said Frida.

"Good-bye, honey," said Mrs. Cat.

"Have a good day. Work hard!"

Mr. Cat and Frida

went down the hill

to the train station.

Mr. Cat paid for two tickets

to the city.

He bought a *Supercat* comic for Frida

and a newspaper for himself.

They waited on the platform

with many other cats.

They were all going

to work in the city, too.

Soon the train came down the track.

"Hurry up, Dad!" said Frida.

"There aren't enough seats

for all these cats!"

Frida found two empty seats.

The train rolled out of the station.

"Tickets please!"

called the conductor.

Frida gave him their tickets.

"Thank you, miss," said the conductor.

Frida read her comic book.

She looked out the window.

They came to the next station.

"Hot potatoes!" said Frida.

"More cats! Where will they sit?"

"They will squeeze on, somehow,"

said Mr. Cat.

Then the train crossed a river

and went into a tunnel.

At last it stopped

at a giant station

in the middle of the city.

"Stay close to me, now,"

said Mr. Cat.

"I am right behind you, Dad!"

said Frida.

She and her father

walked past many tall buildings.

There were huge trees

growing inside some of them.

14

Frida saw a policecat on a horse.

"This is where I work,"

said Mr. Cat.

A sign over the door said

Flying Cat Airlines.

"Which floor, Daddy?"

asked Frida.

"Six," said Mr. Cat.

Frida pressed 6.

Up they went.

The doors opened.

Frida jumped off the elevator—

right into a lady cat

with a watering can.

"Goodness!" said the lady.

"I want to water my plants,

not a little cat.

You must be Frida."

"Frida Cat," said Frida.

"I am Doris," said the lady.

"Your dad and I work together."

"I am going to work here, too,"

said Frida.

She followed her father

into his office.

"What can I do to help, Dad—

I mean, Boss?" Frida asked.

"Hmm. Let me see," said Mr. Cat.

"I know! I have to talk

to Captain Whiskers

about a new plane he is flying.

You may answer my telephone

while I am gone.

Here is a pad

for you to write messages on."

"That will be easy," said Frida.

"Don't worry about your office.

I will take care of everything."

"I am sure you will," said Mr. Cat.

Frida opened the drawers

in her father's desk.

She put a pen behind her ear.

She put some paper clips and tape

inside her pockets.

She popped a candy in her mouth.

Then she put some paper

into the typewriter.

She wrote,

Dear Mommy,
How are you?
I am having fun.
There ~~a~~ is a picture
of me on Daddy's desk.
And there is a
picture of you in
that old black dress
you hate!
Love,
Frida

Frida put her letter

in a big yellow envelope.

She wrote her address on the front.

Next she found a rubber stamp

and put *Handle with Care*

all over it.

Just then the telephone rang.

"Hello?" said Frida.

"This is Daddy's office.

I mean,

this is Mr. Cat's office.

What did you say?

Thank you. Good-bye."

Frida wrote on the pad,

Doris came to the door.

"Do you need anything, Frida?"

"I would like to mail this letter

to my mother," said Frida.

"Sure," said Doris. "Follow me."

Frida and Doris went down a hall.

"This is the chute for letters,"

said Doris.

Frida put her letter in the slot.

Whoosh! Down it went.

"It will fall all the way

to the mail room

in the basement," Doris said.

"I hope it won't get stuck,"

said Frida.

She went back to Mr. Cat's office.

The phone rang again.

"This is Frida Cat," said Frida.

"May I help you? I see. Uh-huh.

Thank you. Good-bye."

28

She wrote on the pad,

Call Harry Snarl right away!

Then she drew a picture.

"That is very good," said Doris.

"Would you like to make

a copy for your mother?"

"Sure!" said Frida.

Doris and Frida

went to the copy machine.

They put Frida's picture

on some glass.

"How many copies

would you like to make?" Doris asked.

"Three," said Frida.

"One for Daddy,

one for Mommy,

and one for you!"

"How nice!" Doris said.

"Press down three, then."

Frida pressed the 3.

She pressed it again,

just to make sure.

The machine made 33 copies

of Frida's picture.

"Oh-oh," said Doris.

Frida looked around.

She taped a picture

on the copy machine.

She put one on the ladies' room door
and another on the men's room door.
She put her picture . . . everywhere.

Back in Mr. Cat's office,

Frida found a note.

It said,

To: FRIDA C.
From: YOUR FATHER
ARE YOU FREE FOR
LUNCH? I WOULD
LIKE TO TAKE YOU
TO THE TOP OF THE
WORLD. BUT FIRST
I MUST GO TO A
MEETING.
MEET ME HERE
    AT 12:00

"Gosh, I wish *I* could go

to the Top of the World,"

said a voice behind her.

"Who are you?" asked Frida.

"Greg Pussywillow,"

said a spotted cat.

"I pass out the mail.

Would you like

an old marshmallow?"

"Thank you, no," said Frida.

"Can I help pass out the mail?"

"Sure. Hop on," said Greg.

Frida jumped on the cart.

First Greg pushed Frida

down the hall.

Then Frida pushed Greg.

She went faster and faster.

"Oh-oh. Sorry."

Frida and Greg

came to a door that said

H. Snarl, President.

"We can't go in there!"

warned Greg.

"Mr. Snarl has an awful temper!"

It was too late.

Frida had opened the door.

There was her father!

"Hi, Daddy—I mean, Boss!"

Frida called.

"Uh—please wait outside, Frida,"

said Mr. Cat.

"Is that Frida Cat?"

asked Mr. Snarl.

"Yes," said Frida.

"Where are your Flying Cat wings?"

asked Mr. Snarl.

"I don't have any," said Frida.

"Now you do," said Mr. Snarl.

He pinned a set of wings

on Frida's blouse.

"Welcome to Flying Cat Airlines,"

he said.

"Thank you, sir."

"You had better go, now,"

said Mr. Cat.

Frida left Mr. Snarl's office.

She closed the door.

" 'Fraidy cat!" she said

to Greg Pussywillow.

At last it was 12 o'clock.

The Top of the World Restaurant

was on the twenty-fifth floor.

"I have never been

twenty-five floors high before!"

Frida said.

"Table for two?

Come this way,"

said the head waiter.

"Wow! Look at that, Dad,"

said Frida.

Another waiter gave Frida

a huge menu with fancy writing.

It took her a long time

to read it all.

"Can I have a double liverburger

with french fries and catnip?"

she asked.

"That *does* look good," said Mr. Cat.

"I will have the same thing.

Now, what should we do

this afternoon?"

"I will help some more, Daddy,"

said Frida. "I already know

how to type letters

and take phone messages

and pass out mail

and make lots of copies of things."

"What about a movie, instead?"

asked Mr. Cat.

"Really?" said Frida.

"What would we see?"

"We could see

Invasion of the Kitten Snatchers,"

said Mr. Cat.

"Hooray!" said Frida.

"That will be even more fun

than working!"

After lunch,

Mr. Cat put some papers

in his briefcase.

"I will look at these

on the train," he told Doris.

"'Bye, everyone!" said Frida.

"We will have to take a subway

to get to the movie," said Mr. Cat.

They went down some stairs

into the ground.

Mr. Cat bought two tokens.

Frida put one in a slot.

Then she pushed the turnstile—hard.

Cats and trains

rushed back and forth.

Mr. Cat and Frida

stepped on a train

that was going downtown.

It was very loud!

53

Frida held on tight.

A cat was singing.

Another was sleeping in a corner.

A lame cat begged for money.

Mr. Cat gave him two coins.

"Poor cat," he said.

When the train got to Eighth Street,

Mr. Cat and Frida got off.

They ran to the theater.

The movie would start soon.

"Would you like some popcorn,
or would you like a soda?"
asked Mr. Cat.
"Both," said Frida.

It was a good movie.

Mr. Cat gasped

when all the kittens

turned into vegetables.

Frida held his paw

so he wouldn't be scared.

After the show,

Mr. Cat and Frida

took a walk to the river.

They saw a helicopter land

next to an old sailing ship.

Mr. Cat bought Frida

a little bottle with a ship in it.

Frida bought two big mouse balloons

for her mother and father.

Soon it was dark.

"Now we must hurry," said Mr. Cat,

"or we will miss our train!"

They took a taxi to the station.

Everyone was rushing to be home.

On the train,

Mr. Cat opened his briefcase.

He took out some papers.

Then he fell asleep.

Frida woke him at their stop.

"Whew—I am tired!" said Mr. Cat.

"I am not tired," said Frida.

"It was fun to work at your office."

Mr. Cat smiled.

"You call that fun?" he said.

"All that work, work, work?"

"You silly Boss—

I mean, Daddy!" said Frida.

She gave him a hug.

Then she saw Mrs. Cat

waiting for them.

"Hi, Mommy!" Frida called,

and she ran to tell her mother

all about her day.